THE LITTLE
RED PEN

THE LITTLE RED PEN

Written by Janet Stevens and Susan Stevens Crummel

Illustrated by Janet Stevens

Houghton Mifflin Harcourt

Boston New York

"Let's get to work!"

The Little Red Pen whirled about—
checking, circling, and marking out.

"There's too much to do!
Where are my helpers?
Stapler, **Scissors**, Pencil,
Eraser, Pushpin, Highlighter!
Are you hiding in the drawer?
Get up here *now!*
If the papers aren't graded,
the students won't learn.
The school might close.
The walls might tumble.
The floors might crumble.
The sky might fall.
It might be
the end of the
world!

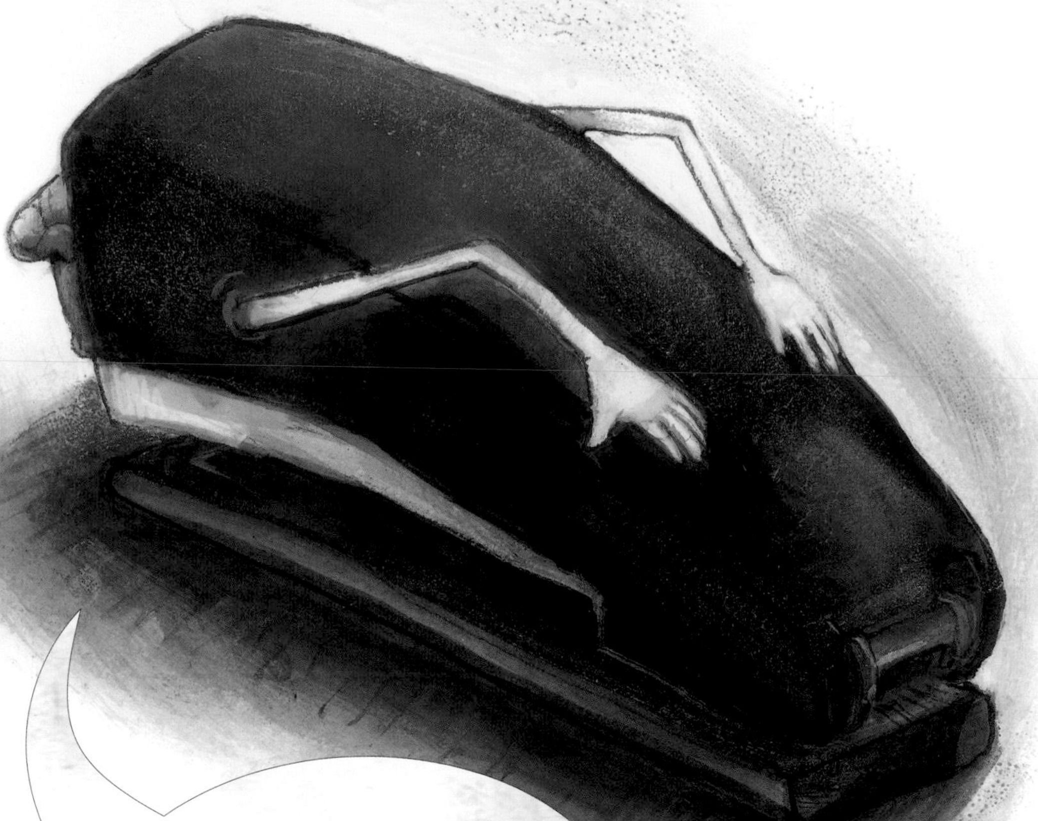
My back is killing me! Everybody keeps pounding on it. I could break!

I write all day, and what do I get? Sharpened down to a nub. Who needs a nub?

Don't call me Pushpin. My name is Señorita Chincheta. And I am *la última chincheta*. If I get lost—no more *chinchetas*. *¿Comprende?*

I've been cutting up all day. I'm getting dull. Not good for a sharp guy like me!
What was the question? I forget everything. My head is shrinking.
I'm bright, not crazy! Remember Mr. Felt-Tip Marker? His cap was left off, and you know where he ended up.

"The Pit of No Return!"
everyone cried.

"THE TRASH."

"Rubbish!" The Little Red Pen frowned. "You can't spend your life hiding, worrying about the Pit. There's work to be done, and I need help!"

"**Well, Big Bossy Ballpoint,**" said Scissors, "**why don't you ask Tank? He'd be a huge help.**"

"Tank? That lazy hamster? Never!" said the Little Red Pen. "The papers must be graded. I'll have to do it myself!"

And so she did.
Well, she tried.

Scritch

Scratch

Scritch

The Little Red Pen worked long into the night. In the wee hours of the morning she could barely move across the page.

She wibbled. She wobbled.

Scritch

Scratch   Scritch

Then she fell over, exhausted. The Little Red Pen began to

r-r-r-r-r-r-o-l-l-l-l-l-l-l-l . . . . . right to the edge of the desk.

"What was that?" yelled Stapler.

"The sky is falling!" cried Pencil. "It's the end of the world!"

"No, it's not," said Highlighter. "It's probably Tank moving around in his cage."

Scissors rolled his eyes. "No way! Big Boy never moves."

"It *is* the end!" said Pencil. "I heard Pen say it. What are we going to do?"

"We're going up," snipped Scissors. "Get the lead out, Stubby!"

"Yeah," said Eraser. "Let's go . . . go . . . Where are we going? I forgot."

"To the desktop!" Chincheta shouted. "*¡Vámonos! ¡Arriba, arriba!*"

"*¡Ay, caramba! Muchos* papers!"

"Pen's *gone!*" cried Pencil. "And the papers aren't finished! The students won't learn! It's the end of the world!"

"It is *not* the end of the world," muttered Stapler.

"How do we know for sure?" asked Highlighter. "The papers have always been graded. Who knows what will happen if they're not?"

"I know!" said Eraser.

"WHAT?" They all glared.

"I forgot."

Scissors shook his head. "The end of the world could be worse than the Pit. The papers must be graded. We'll have to do it ourselves!"

And so they did.

Well, they tried.

Scissors grabbed a paper.

"No capital letter!" Clip.

"Dot that *i*!" Snip.

"Not like that!" Stapler groaned. "You cut it to shreds. Let me do it! Eraser, hop on. I see a mis-spelled word!" Bam! "This sentence needs a verb!" Bam! "This whole paragraph is wrong!" Bam bam bam bam bam bam!

"Not like THAT," said Highlighter. "Too many staples! Let me do it!"

Squeak squeak squeak-e-e-e-e

"Not like that!" Eraser squinted. "Too bright! Let me do it!"

Rubbity rub smudgity smudge

"Not like that, numbskull," said Scissors. "You erased everything! Even the student's name! Whose paper is this?"

"I forgot," moaned Eraser.

They rushed to the edge of the desk.

"**Oh, no,**" whispered Eraser. "**Pen is in the . . . the . . .**"

"*¡El pozo de no returno!*" shouted Chincheta.

Pencil broke down. "What are we going to do? We need her. If the papers aren't graded, the students won't learn. Then they—"

"**Oh, stop it already,**" Stapler grumbled.

"I hate to be blunt," said Scissors, "but she's a goner. No one comes back from the Pit."

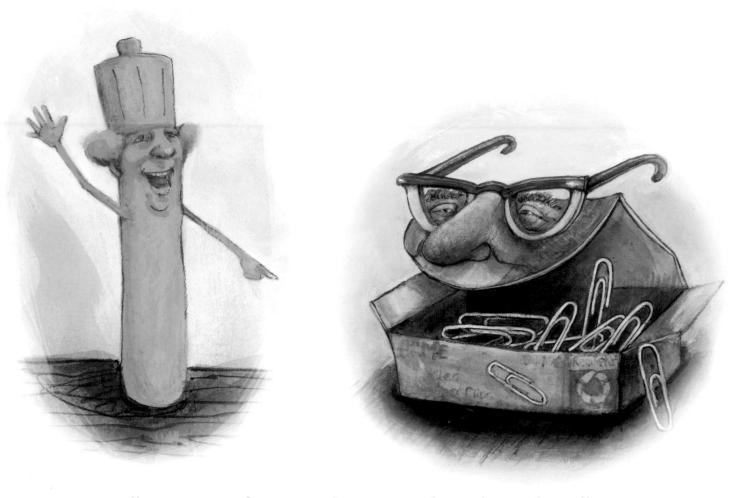

"Not so fast. I have a bright idea,"
said Highlighter. "Paper Clip Box! Where
are you? Give me your clips."

"Can't have 'em." Box scowled. "Without my clips,
I'm empty. Useless. I'll end up in the—"

"OUT WITH THE CLIPS!" yelled
Highlighter. "We need a chain!"

One by one,   the paper clips marched out   and hooked together.

"**I know what to do!**" Eraser grabbed the chain and raced across the desktop. Then he forgot to stop, bounced off the edge, and . . .

Clunk!

Hey, everybody! Guess who's down here in the Pit? The Little Red . . . uh . . . what's-her-face!

We know, rubbernoggin. Now you're both in the Pit.

"I have another bright idea," said Highlighter. "Eraser, grab the Little Red Pen. We'll pull you both up. Ready, everybody?"

"Too heavy." Scissors panted. "Any more bright ideas?"

"Yes!" cried Highlighter. "The hamster wheel! We'll hook the chain to the wheel! Then Tank will run, the wheel will turn, the chain will—"

"Whoa," Scissors cut in. "Tanky Boy hasn't been on the wheel in years. Besides, how are we going to get from here to there?"

"Ruler can be our bridge!" declared Highlighter.

"What? Me, a bridge?" Ruler snapped. "I'm not budging an inch."

"Move it!" yelled Highlighter.

"Oh, all right." Ruler stretched out. Farther . . .
farther . . . one more inch . . . half an inch . . .

Clunk!

Oh, great. Three in the Pit.

Need some help?
Yardstick! I thought you were broken and down in the—

"The Pit?" said Yardstick. "Nobody throws me in the Pit. I may be shorter now, but I'm tall enough to hold up this plant and long enough to be your bridge."

Yardstick stretched out. Farther . . . farther . . . one more inch . . . half an inch . . . He made it!

Everyone dashed across, but Pencil froze.
"I—I—I'm afraid."

"Aw, come on, Pencil! You can do it!"
said Stapler. "Don't look down!"

Sharpener peeked out from under a pile of
papers. "I'll help you."

"Ahhhhhh!" Pencil took one look at
Sharpener and bolted across.

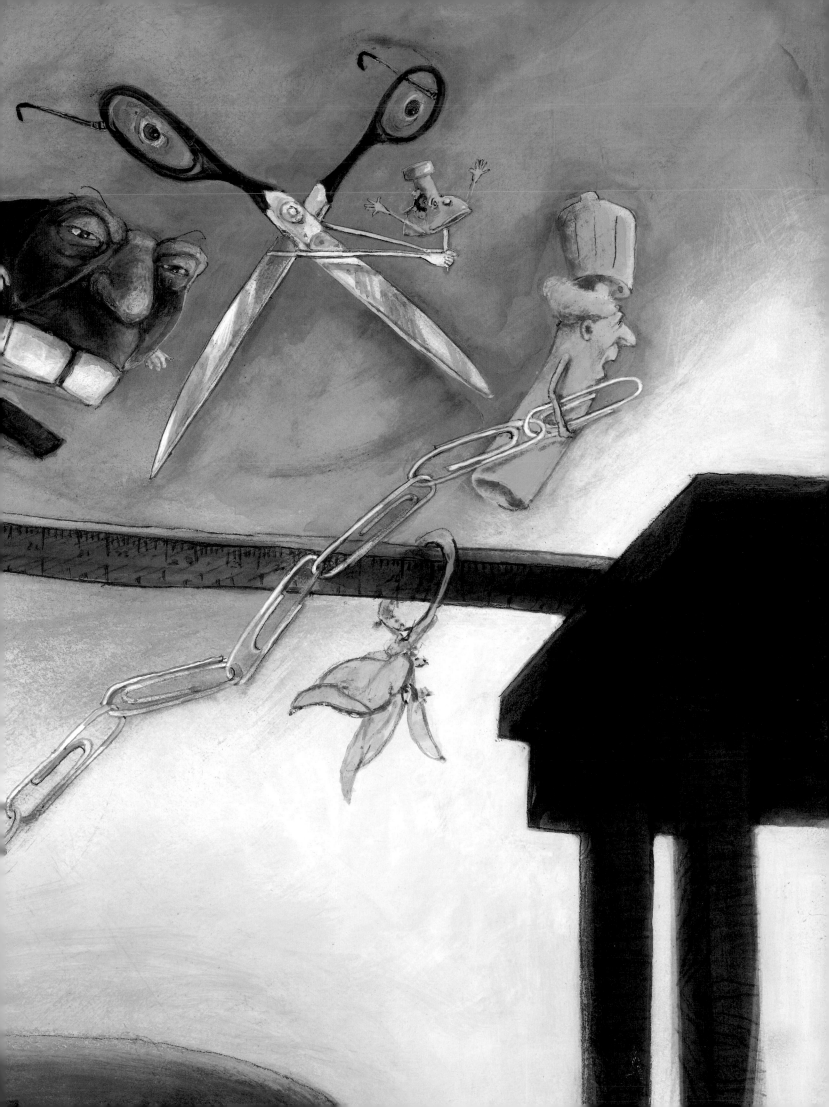

snort snort

z-z-z-z-z-z-z-z-z-z-z-z-z-z-z-z-z-z-z-z-z-z-z-z

They opened the cage door and crept inside. Highlighter hooked the paper clip chain to the wheel. **"Okay. Grab Tank. We're hauling him over."**

"Hamster *grande*," Chincheta groaned. "¡MUY *grande!*"

They huffed and they puffed until finally they pulled Tank onto the wheel.

Highlighter took a deep breath. "Wake up, Tank! Run!"

snort. z-z-z-z-z-z-z-z-z-z-z-z-z-z-z

Chincheta smiled.

"I can wake him up."

POKE! ROARRRRRRRR!

"Tankzilla!" Pencil shrieked.
"It's the end of the world!"

Around and around.

Faster and faster.

The wheel turned.

The chain moved.

Up. Up. Up.

Up came **Ruler**.

Up came **Eraser**.

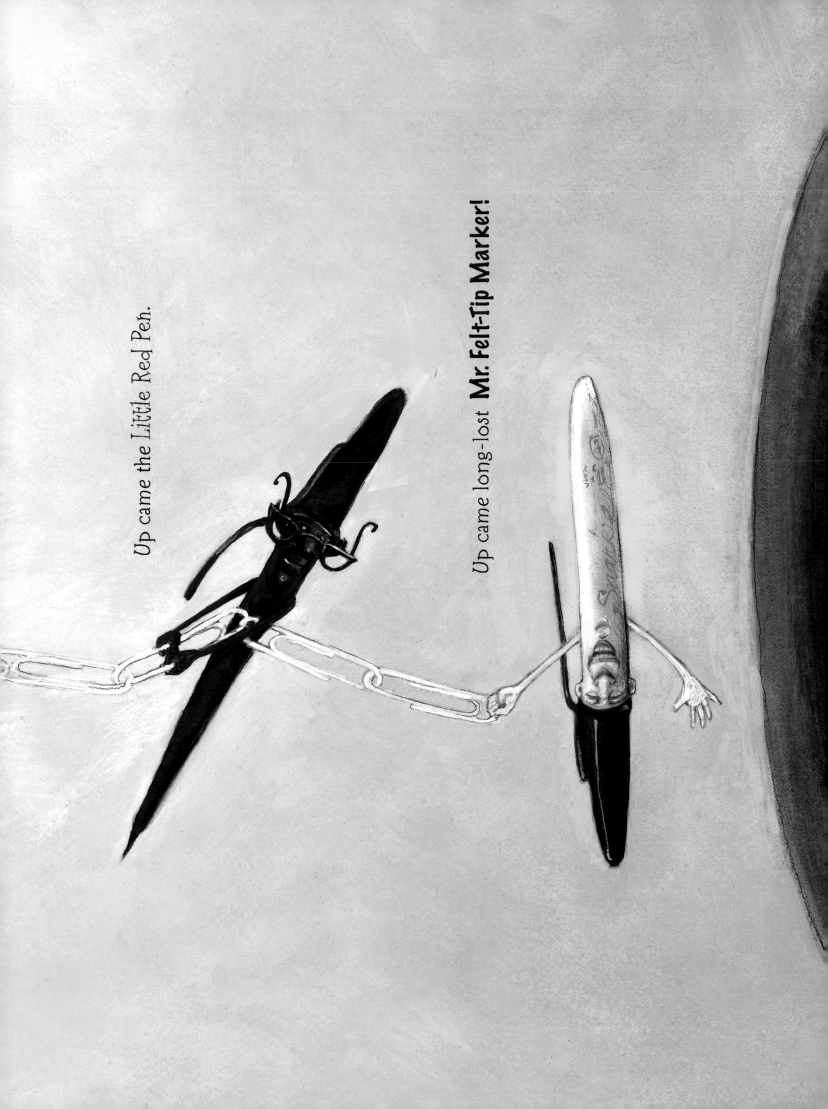

Up came the Little Red Pen.

Up came long-lost **Mr. Felt-Tip Marker!**

"It worked!" shouted Highlighter. "And we did it all by ourselves!"

Chincheta clapped. "¡Bravo!"

"Did we save the world?" asked Pencil.

The Little Red Pen beamed. "You saved us, but now—"

"**Now,**" said Eraser, "**we have a job to finish!**"

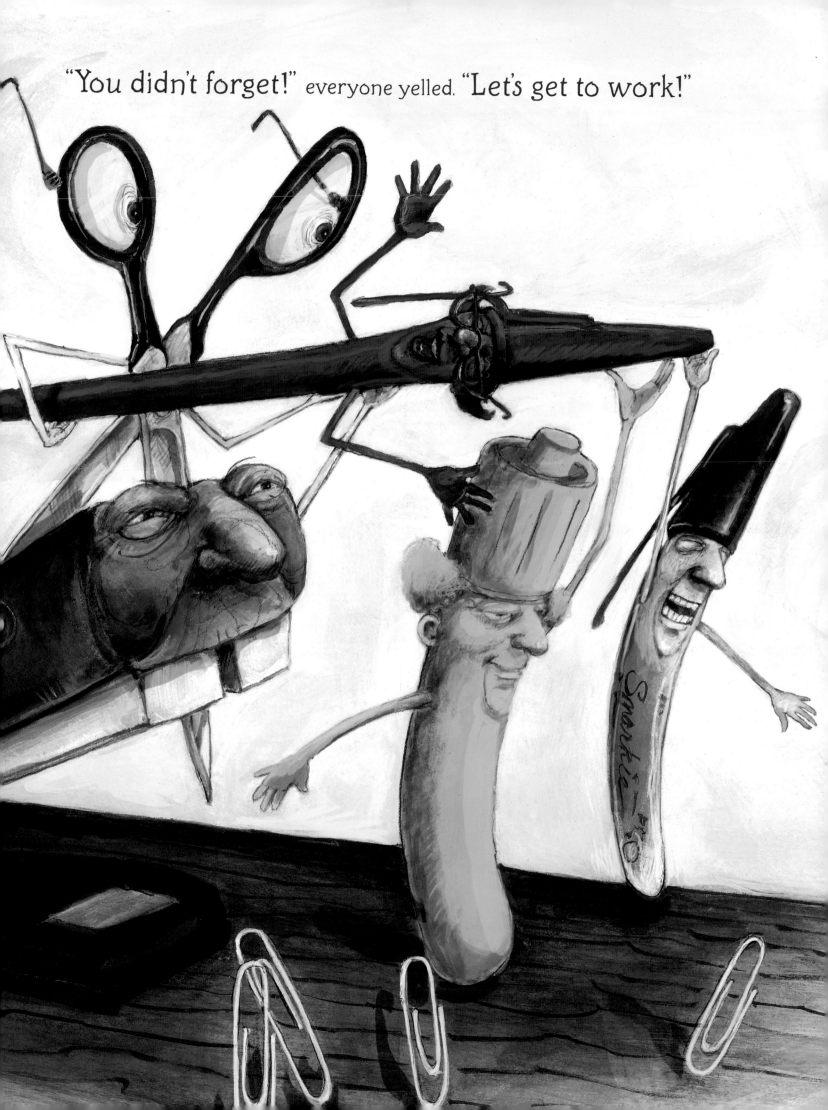

And so they did. They checked and stapled, organized and alphabetized, piled and filed, without another thought of running low, becoming dull, drying up, getting lost, breaking down, or landing in the Pit until the job was done.

The world was safe.

And no one hid in the drawer ever again.

Except you-know-who.

To Jeannnette, the real little Pen Red
and a great editor
—Janet and Susan

hmhbooks.com

The illustrations in this book were done in mixed media.

Designed by Regina Roff.

The Library of Congress has cataloged the hardcover edition as follows:

Stevens, Janet.
The little red pen / written by Janet Stevens and Susan Stevens Crummel; illustrated by Janet
Stevens. p. cm.
Summary: When a little red pen accidentally falls into the waste basket while trying
to correct papers all by herself, the other classroom supplies must cooperate to
rescue her.[1. Office equipment and supplies—Fiction. 2. Schools—Fiction. 3.
Humorous stories.] I. Crummel, Susan Stevens. II. Title. PZ7.S84453Li 2011
[E]—dc22
2010009062

ISBN: 978-0-15-206432-7 hardcover
ISBN: 978-0-358-13730-6 paperback

Printed in Italy
7
4500837046